Tick Tock

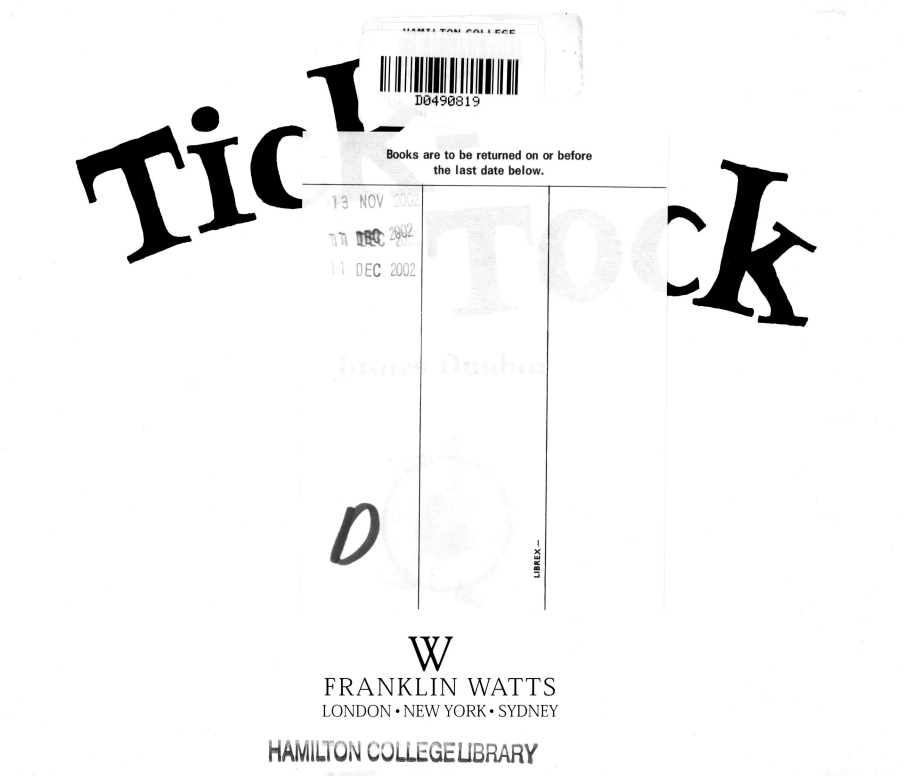

James Dunbar

W
FRANKLIN WATTS
LONDON · NEW YORK · SYDNEY

This book is about something we cannot see, hear, touch or smell.
It is something we all have a sense of and we all have to live with.
It is............

............so old it must have started before the world was created
and it has carried on ever since, right up until now. And it will
probably keep on going, perhaps for ever and ever. It is.............

something that can help us measure the speed of a shooting star,
yet also show us how slowly a snail crawls or a plant grows. It ....

..........helps us to understand how long ago dinosaurs lived or
how many days there are before our birthday. It is..............

TIME.

Put your hands on your heart. Feel it beat, Tick-Tock, just like a clock. With every heartbeat about a second of TIME passes.

Count your heartbeats...
one, two, three,
four, five...

We can try measuring TIME in heartbeats.

What can happen in ten heartbeats?

In ten heartbeats a snail can crawl the length of your hand...

...try standing on one leg for twenty heartbeats...

...in twenty-five heartbeats an ant can run across two pages...

...for how many heartbeats can you balance a book on your head?

Your heart is always beating, Tick-Tock, Tick-Tock and TIME is passing.

But there is a problem...

Our heart does not always beat at the same speed. It beats quickly when we run, and slowly when we rest or sleep. So counting heartbeats is not an accurate way to measure TIME.

This is an egg timer. The sand trickles from the top to the bottom in the TIME it takes to boil an egg.

Marks on a candle can measure TIME as the candle burns down.

A clock is our best way of measuring TIME... there are...

clocks and watches we can carry with us... clocks to wake us up... clocks for lots of people to see.

Clocks measure TIME in seconds, minutes and hours.

7

When a clock goes Tick-Tock about one SECOND of TIME has passed.
We use seconds to measure TIME that happens quickly.

One second is about as long as a sneeze...

In fifteen seconds a fly can beat its wings about five hundred times...
... how many times can you flap your arms up and down in that time?

an apple takes about two seconds to fall from a tall tree.

Flying fish can stay in the air for up to twenty seconds...

forty seconds to get completely washed and dressed seems very little time.

In fifty seconds a snail can crawl nearly the length of one page!

Try staring into someone's eyes without blinking for forty seconds.

And still TIME goes on, Tick-Tock, Tick-Tock. Now sixty seconds has ticked away, that makes one minute. What can happen in one minute?

We use MINUTES to measure TIME that takes a bit longer to pass.

There is more TIME for things to happen in minutes.

It will take between four and five minutes to empty a bath full of water.

If you talk for two minutes you can say between two hundred and three hundred words.

10

Now you are getting better at measuring minutes guess how many minutes it takes to...

Thirty minutes is about two thousand heartbeats but who's counting?
How many different things can I do in fifty minutes?

draw a picture of yourself...

...to watch your favourite TV show.

When sixty minutes have ticked away that will make one hour.

We use HOURS to measure longer periods of TIME.

In one hour most people can walk two or three kilometres.

Think of all the TIME you spend sitting down to eat.
It adds up to more than two hours each day.

In eighteen hours a cat drinks about half a litre of milk or water... an elephant drinks about one thousand litres of water.

In twenty hours some tropical grasses can grow twenty-five centimetres.

When twenty-four hours have passed that is one day.

There is enough time in one DAY
to do many things.

In one day there is daylight and night time.
We divide up the TIME in a day into
morning, afternoon, evening and night.

Night is for sleeping.

When we are asleep TIME still ticks on.
But in our sleep we have no sense of TIME.

We seem to dream things in no TIME at all. We can fly to the moon and back.... and we may be chased by monsters!

When we wake up we have no idea how long we have been asleep. It is morning and another day begins.

How do we keep count of the days?

15

The clock carries on ticking and TIME goes on day after day. To count the days we look at a calendar.

The calendar shows us there are seven days.

We do different things on each day. But there are some things we do everyday.

Monday

Tuesday

Wednesday

watch television

play with friends

read a book

Thursday

Friday

go shopping

make a mess

Saturday

be happy

Sunday

give someone a hug or feed a pet!

Add these seven days together and we have one week.
Where does TIME go from here?

There are twelve MONTHS.

The calendar tells us the name of each month and the order they come in.

We can write on the calendar what is going to happen in each month...

In which month is your birthday?

January

February

March

April

May

June

July

When do you go on holiday?

August

September

October

November

December

In one month you will have gone to bed and woken up about thirty times...

Some months have festivals and celebrations when everyone has fun.

We join up twelve months and call them one YEAR.

When twelve months have passed the world is one year older and still our heart is going Tick-Tock.

In one year there are...

three hundred and sixty-fiv

Days

about thirty-one million and five hundred thousand

Seconds

which is

which is about

eight thousand and seven hundr

Hours

five hundred and twenty-five thousand

Minutes

which is about

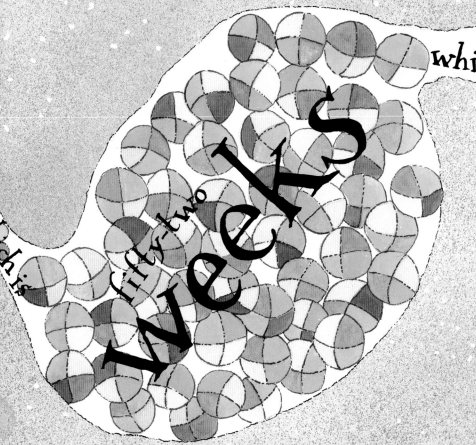

which is

fifty-two weeKs

which is

twelve Months

which is

one Year

Imagine that when the year is over we could put all this TIME into a large box.

When one year ends, a new one begins. We give each one a number. The new year will have the next number.

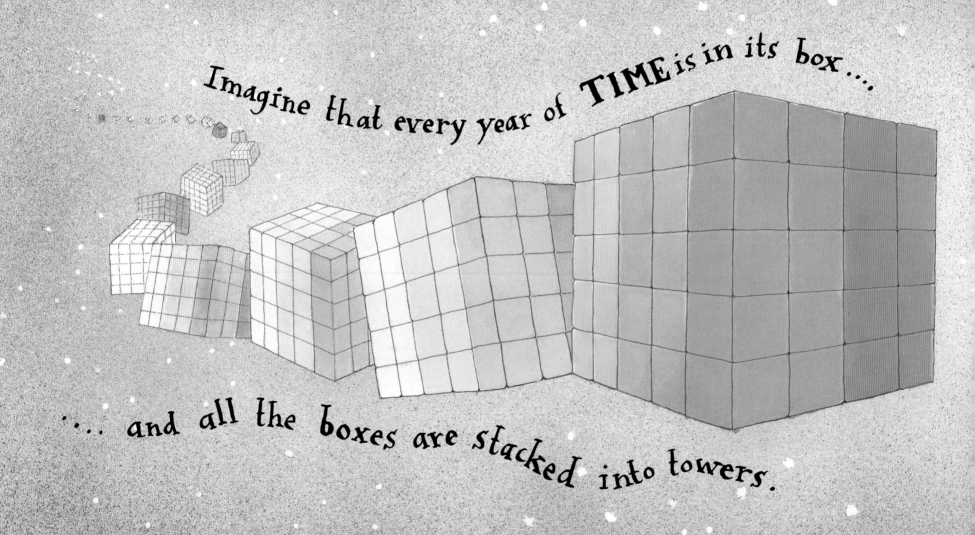

Imagine that every year of **TIME** is in its box ....

.... and all the boxes are stacked into towers.

Ten years are called a DECADE... one hundred years are called a CENTURY.

When a century has ended a new century begins.

SPRING

SUMMER

As TIME moves on through the year we see changes in the world around us. These changes are called the SEASONS of the year. In each year there are four seasons.

AUTUMN

WINTER

When these four seasons are over, they begin again. And
so the seasons go on year after year...

As TIME ticks on, year after year, everything gets older.

But clocks and calendars cannot always tell us how old something is.

Sometimes we have to use our sense of TIME.

We can sense how old something is by how it changes.

six weeks

six months

two years

Sometimes we can guess how old a thing is by how it looks.

29

The TIME when there were dinosaurs on Earth has passed, millions of years ago.

The TIME when you were a baby has passed a few years ago.

All this TIME is in the PAST.

30

The TIME when you will finish this book will be soon...

then there will be all the TIME which has not yet happened.

All this TIME is in the FUTURE.

As you hold this book, read this page and look at the picture... the TIME is NOW.

And your heart is still going Tick-Tock.

First published in 1996 by Franklin Watts
This paperback edition published in 1997
This edition 1998

Franklin Watts, 96 Leonard Street, London EC2A 4RH
Franklin Watts Australia, 14 Mars Road, Lane Cove, NSW 2066

Text and illustrations © 1996 James Dunbar

Series editor: Paula Borton
Art director: Robert Walster
Design consultant: Richard Langford

A CIP catalogue record for this book is available from the British Library

ISBN 0 7496 2753 0 (paperback)
     0 7496 2329 2 (hardback)

Dewey classification 529

Printed in Singapore